DISNEP
FROZEN

Special Edition
Junior Novelization

[handwritten signatures]

randomhousekids.com

ISBN 978-0-7364-3296-2

Printed in the United States of America

10 9 8 7 6 5 4 3 2 1

Special Edition
Junior Novelization

Adapted by Sarah Nathan and Sela Roman

Random House 🏠 New York

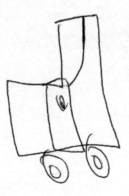

Prologue

$\mathscr{L}$ong ago, atop a mountain high above the kingdom of Arendelle, a group of strong men were hard at work. They were ice harvesters, men who cut and hauled huge blocks of ice from the mountain lakes. Horses stood at attention, waiting with empty wagons to be filled. The ice blocks were hoisted into the wagons; soon they would be taken down to the village to sell. It was a dangerous business. One slip could send a block hurtling down the mountainside—or even worse, falling on a man and crushing him.

A boy stood in the shadows watching the workmen. He kept a small sled at his side. His name was Kristoff, and he desperately wanted to join the ice harvesters, but he was too young. Standing next to him was his friend Sven, a baby reindeer. Kristoff imagined the two of them taking a sled full of ice blocks into the village of Arendelle. Sven sniffed the cold air and glanced at the big blocks of ice. They looked very heavy. He snorted but didn't move a hoof.

As evening approached, Kristoff finally convinced Sven to carry a small load of ice on their sled. By now, the men had lit several lanterns and were finishing loading their own wagons. Kristoff crept forward and was able to grab a small block of ice. He finally wrestled the block onto his sled and attached Sven's harness.

Wagon by wagon, the ice harvesters headed down the mountain roads. Kristoff trailed behind with Sven, steering his own small wagon down the bumpy path.

Above them all, the northern lights spread across the dark sky, creating waves of gossamer green light. The magical glow pulsed as it rolled over the mountains, down toward the kingdom below.

In a grassy valley next to a deep fjord, the castle of Arendelle lay silent in the night. The bright luster of the northern lights danced across the windows, waking a small girl. She sat up and grinned to see the wonderful green light.

The girl jumped out of bed and tiptoed across the room to wake her older sister. "Elsa, Elsa!" she said urgently. "Wake up!"

Elsa, who was eight years old, grumbled and ducked under the covers. "Anna, go back to sleep."

But Anna wouldn't give up. "I just can't. The sky's awake, so I'm awake, and so we have to play," she said. "Do you want to build a snowman?"

Elsa's eyes popped open. That got her attention.

The girls were the daughters of Arendelle's king and queen, and the best of friends. Elsa couldn't resist Anna's begging. The sisters ran down the hallway in their nightgowns, laughing as they hurried along. Entering the Great Hall, where all the royal balls were held, they turned to each other.

"Are you ready?" Elsa asked, smiling.

"Yes, yes!" Anna cried, reaching out to tickle her sister.

Elsa giggled, and suddenly, snowflakes seemed to burst in a flurry from her hands!

Anna clapped happily. She knew that her sister had a very special talent: she could create snow and ice, even in the middle of summer!

With a twirl and a wave of her hands, Elsa magically summoned her icy powers. Quickly, she filled the Great Hall with mounds of fluffy snow, turning it into a winter playground. Then she stomped her feet and ice swept across the floor. She laughed to see little Anna hopping around joyfully.

Together, they went to work building their snowman. Anna did her best to roll out the snowman's body. Then she ran to get a carrot for the nose. "Snowman!" she exclaimed proudly.

Elsa laughed at the lopsided snowman. "Hi, I'm Olaf," she said in a deep voice, pretending to be the snowman. "And I like warm hugs."

The girls danced around their funny snowman.

Then Elsa gathered her icy magic and made a swooping ice slide. Anna squealed with delight. She climbed to the top of the slide, then zoomed down and soared up again along the icy curve. Elsa quickly created another slide to catch Anna as she came down. The little girl gained speed and was tossed upward again. Elsa had to work fast to keep pace with Anna. She kept making more slides so her sister could stay aloft as she flew around the room.

"Anna, slow down," Elsa said, starting to get worried. "It's too high!"

But Anna was having fun. The little princess was fearless, jumping and sliding to each new slide as quickly as Elsa made it. Elsa raised her hand to create the next slide, but suddenly, her foot slipped. As she stumbled, her magic went awry. Her frozen blast caught the side of Anna's head, right through her curls.

Anna gasped and fell to the ground, unconscious.

"Anna!" Elsa shouted, running to her sister. She lifted Anna up and felt her cold, shivering body. A lock of Anna's hair had turned pure white where the magic had hit it. "Mama! Papa!" Elsa cried desperately.

As she called for help and her worry increased, icicles formed on the ceiling, and frozen spikes grew tall around the girls.

The king and queen burst into the Great Hall to find their daughters huddled in a frozen landscape. They knew that Elsa had a special ability to create ice, but this was more than they'd ever seen. "Elsa," the king cried. "This is getting out of hand!"

"I'm sorry," Elsa replied in distress. "I didn't mean it!"

"Anna!" the queen gasped, and ran toward her little girl.

2

The castle's library was dark, but the king knew what he was looking for: an ancient book filled with knowledge from centuries past. When he found it, he pulled it from the shelf and quickly flipped through the pages to the section he needed. In it was a drawing of a troll, which seemed to be holding the northern lights in its hands. In front of the troll, a wounded human lay quiet while the troll used the magic of the northern lights to heal him. The king turned the page and spotted a crumbling document tucked into the book. He carefully unfolded the yellowed map.

Wasting no time, the king and queen threw on their cloaks, bundled up their daughters, and ordered that the horses be saddled. The royal family hurried away from the castle. The queen traveled on her own horse with Elsa, while the king held Anna in his arms. The horses thundered up the mountain path.

Kristoff and Sven were walking down the rocky mountain path under the bright glow of the northern lights. But as the rumble of hooves filled the air, they moved aside, wary of the approaching horses. They watched the riders gallop past, leaving a trail of ice behind them.

Curious, Kristoff and Sven followed the travelers to a ridge above a mountain valley. The two hid behind a rock and watched as the horses whinnied and came to a stop.

The king and queen dismounted. The king held a young girl to his shoulder; the queen held the hand of a slightly older girl.

"Please, help!" the king cried out. "My daughter!"

The hillside appeared empty at first. Then a pile of rocks rolled down the hillside. Suddenly, the rocks unfolded themselves into legs and arms and stood up, revealing themselves to be small gray creatures— they weren't rocks at all! "Trolls," Kristoff whispered to Sven.

At that moment, a rock next to Kristoff jumped up, turning into a short troll woman covered with moss. Her name was Hulda.

"Shush," Hulda told Kristoff absently. "I'm trying

to listen." Then, startled, Hulda looked more closely at Kristoff, realizing for the first time that he was not a troll. Her face broke into a grin, and she reached out to give Kristoff and Sven big hugs. "Cuties!" she said, laughing.

In the valley, the king stood with his daughters as Pabbie, a very old troll, made his way through the crowd to gaze at the princesses.

First he looked at Elsa. "Was she born with the powers or cursed?" he asked.

"Born," the king answered. "And they're getting stronger."

The troll then turned his attention to Anna, who was still unconscious. "You are lucky it wasn't her heart that was struck," he noted. "The heart is not so easily changed, but the head can be persuaded." He paused. "We should remove all the magic, even memories of magic, to be safe."

The king nodded. "Do what you must," he said.

With a gentle touch of his fingers, the troll pulled a series of glowing memories from little Anna's head. The memories hovered in the air as the troll transformed them into more sensible scenes. Instead of a magical snowman in the ballroom, Anna would

9

now remember a winter scene in the courtyard. Instead of snowflakes in the hallway, she would remember snowflakes falling outside the window. All the magical moments she had shared with Elsa were gone, replaced with normal moments. The only remnant of her magical accident was the streak of white in her hair.

"There," said Pabbie when he was finished. "She will remember the fun, but not the magic."

"She won't remember that I have powers?" Elsa asked.

"No," Pabbie said.

"It's for the best," the king told her.

"Listen to me, Elsa," Pabbie said. "Your power will only grow. There is beauty in it, but also great danger."

As he spoke, the troll conjured up an image of an older Elsa in the sky. The image twirled gracefully, surrounded by beautiful snowflakes.

Then, amid the northern lights, the snowflakes turned into sharp spikes. The spectre of a crowd joined Elsa in the sky—the people used the icy spikes as weapons, attacking Elsa's glowing effigy.

"You must learn to control your power," Pabbie

continued. "Fear will be your enemy."

The king hugged Elsa close. "We'll protect her," he promised. "We'll lock the gates. We'll reduce the staff and keep her powers hidden from everyone . . . including Anna."

3

Back at the castle, the king and queen immediately ordered that the castle gates be locked. All the doors were closed and the windows shuttered. They kept the girls secluded and no longer opened the castle to visitors. The family stayed hidden, tucked away inside their walled kingdom.

The king and queen acted just as cautiously inside the castle. As the princesses grew, their parents did everything they could to ensure that Elsa learned to control herself. That meant the girls were hardly ever together. Nor did Elsa seek Anna out, since she was afraid she might accidentally hurt her. Day after day, Elsa spent most of her time training to be the next ruler—and learning to keep her powers in check.

The training was difficult, and Elsa often felt unable to contain her magic. Ice seemed to form on her fingertips whenever she laughed or cried or became upset.

Worried, the king gave Elsa a pair of leather gloves. He advised her to keep them on at all times, and reminded her that she had to hide her icy magic in order to stay safe. "Conceal it," he told her.

"Don't feel it," she answered.

"Don't let it show," he agreed.

The years slipped by. Anna spent most of her time alone. Sometimes she played with her dolls; sometimes she pretended to have conversations with painted portraits in the gallery. But she was lonely.

Time after time, she knocked on Elsa's door, pleading with her sister to come out and play. But Elsa never did. The memory of their friendship was slowly fading.

One day, Anna peered out her window and saw snow falling in the royal gardens. She raced down the hallway to her sister's room. "Do you want to build a snowman?" she called through the closed door.

There was no reply from inside. The door did not open. Eventually, Anna went out into the courtyard and tried to build a snowman by herself. After rolling out a lopsided ball, she glanced up at Elsa's window and thought she saw someone smiling down at her. But when she looked again, the face was gone.

Without any memory of Elsa's magic, Anna had no idea why she was always alone. Over time, she simply came to accept that her sister's coldness was part of who she was. She didn't know that Elsa was lonely too, and that she missed Anna as much as Anna missed her. Elsa longed to play with Anna but was fearful of the harm her magic might cause by mistake.

"I'm scared," Elsa told her father one day. "It's getting stronger."

"Getting upset only makes it worse," cautioned the king. "Calm down." He reached out to give Elsa a hug.

"No," she said sharply. "Don't touch me."

--->>·->————❁————<·<<··

One day years later, when the girls were teenagers, the king and queen boarded a ship, intending to visit another kingdom. They hugged their daughters goodbye and left them at home, as they had many times before. But this time, the king and queen never returned. A storm engulfed the ship, and they were lost at sea. The kingdom mourned their rulers.

Inside the castle, Anna felt overcome with grief. Not knowing where else to turn, she knocked again on Elsa's door.

"Elsa? Are you okay? I'm right out here," Anna said. But as always, there was no reply. She slid down and sadly rested her head against the door. "It's just you and me now. What are we going to do?"

Inside her room, Elsa felt awful, too. But she could not open the door. Instead, she sat with her back against the closed door, crying silently. All around her, ice and snow filled the room.

In time, the girls became young ladies. But they had grown apart, and Anna felt she barely knew Elsa anymore.

When Elsa turned twenty-one, it was time for her to be crowned the new Queen of Arendelle. The whole kingdom was bustling with excitement. For the first time in ages, and for one day only, the castle gates would be opened to the village and to all the surrounding kingdoms.

It would be a celebration that Arendelle would never forget.

4

On the morning of Elsa's coronation, the heavy gates to the castle were finally opened. All of Arendelle wanted to celebrate the grand occasion. The streets in front of the castle were crowded with townspeople eager to see the new queen.

To add to the excitement, the fjord was filled with ships from other kingdoms, bringing dignitaries from far away. One by one, important people stepped onto Arendelle's docks.

"Welcome to our humble Arendelle," the royal handler called to the visitors. One of the visiting dignitaries was the Duke of Weselton, a small man with white whiskers. Two huge guards followed close behind him, carrying his luggage.

"Ah, Arendelle, our most mysterious trade partner," the Duke said breezily. "Open those gates so I may unlock your secrets and exploit your riches!"

In the distance, Kristoff was making his way down a mountain path. Now grown-up and strong, he and Sven had become true ice harvesters, masters at hauling ice blocks down the mountain. To Kristoff, the coronation was a perfect opportunity to sell ice to the crowds who filled Arendelle.

"A coronation on a hot July day, you know what that means?" he asked Sven, who was harnessed to their rickety ice cart.

The reindeer raised his eyebrows. Sven couldn't talk, but that wasn't a problem for Kristoff. He often spoke for Sven, changing his voice to sound deeper and more reindeer-y.

"I sure do, Kristoff," he declared, as Sven. "By noon I'm going to smell like a barrel of rabid skunks."

"Yes, you will," Kristoff said, talking normally again. He grinned. "But also, people will be needing ice. Lots of ice." He pulled Sven's rope, and the two continued down into the town.

For Anna, the new people and the excitement were a dream come true. For the first time in years, every door in Arendelle was open. No one was shutting her out! She burst through the busy courtyard in front of the castle and practically skipped into town. People everywhere were getting ready for the coronation. She saw banners, a maypole, and flowers—all celebrating her sister, the new queen. There were dancing groups, musical bands, and food stalls. Everything looked so interesting.

"I can't wait to meet everyone!" Anna exclaimed out loud. Then she stopped short as a thought occurred to her. "What if I meet *the one*?" Anna knew she wasn't likely to meet someone special, especially since the castle gates would be open for one day only, exactly twenty-four hours. Still, she couldn't help daydreaming just a bit. Today might be her only chance to meet new friends, have new experiences, and maybe, just maybe, find love.

In her room upstairs in the castle, Elsa did not share the happiness that pulsed through the kingdom. She worried about controlling her powers, and hoped she could just get through the ceremony without anyone learning about her magic.

As a test, she slipped off her gloves and picked up a candlestick and a little jar from the table. She concentrated, holding both with her bare hands. "Be the good girl," Elsa whispered to herself. "Make one wrong move and everyone will know. . . ." She was nervous. As she stood there, ice formed on her palms and moved onto the objects, turning them to ice. She hurriedly dropped them and tugged her gloves back on, concealing her hands—and her icy magic.

"It's only for today," Elsa reminded herself. After that, the gates would be closed again and she could go back into hiding.

5

In the streets below, Anna was strolling dreamily around the harbor, watching the ships and imagining all the fun the coronation party would bring. For once, it wouldn't matter that Elsa didn't want to spend time with her, because she'd be spending time with everyone else!

Anna rounded a corner and suddenly–*smack!*–a horse bumped into her!

Caught by surprise, Anna lost her balance and stumbled, falling into a small rowboat on the dock. The boat tipped precariously toward the water. Luckily, the horse came forward and placed its hoof on the end of the boat to keep it from sliding into the harbor.

"Hey!" Anna exclaimed in surprise, looking up at the horse and its rider.

"I'm so sorry," the rider said. "Are you hurt?"

Anna tried to regain her composure. "Hey, uh . . . No, I'm okay," she managed to say. She couldn't help noticing that the rider was very handsome.

"Are you sure?" the young man asked. He hopped off his horse. He was tall and sharply dressed in a fancy uniform. He looked very concerned about her welfare.

"Yeah, I just wasn't looking where I was going," Anna said. She smiled. "But I'm great, actually."

"Oh, thank goodness," the stranger said, smiling. He stepped into the little boat and extended his hand to Anna. When their eyes met, a happy charge of excitement passed between them.

The young man smiled. "Prince Hans of the Southern Isles," he said, introducing himself.

Anna stood up and curtsied. "Princess Anna of Arendelle," she replied.

"Princess?" he responded, horrified. "My lady!" He dropped to one knee and bowed his head.

His horse also dropped to one knee. Immediately, the little boat tipped backward, and Hans tumbled on top of Anna. They both giggled awkwardly.

"Hi again," Anna said. The prince's face was just inches from hers.

Apparently realizing his mistake, the horse slammed its hoof back down on the boat. Anna and Hans fell the opposite way. This time, Anna landed on top of Hans!

"Oh, boy," Hans said, embarrassed.

"Ha! This is awkward," Anna said, acknowledging their positions. "Not that you're awkward," she said, trying to cover her embarrassment. "But just because we're . . . I'm awkward!" she said. "You're gorgeous." Her hand flew to her mouth. Had she just said that out loud? "Wait, what?"

Hans jumped to his feet, quickly regaining a royal posture. "I'd like to formally apologize for hitting the Princess of Arendelle with my horse. And for every moment after," he added.

"No, no," Anna said. "It's fine. I'm not that princess. I mean, if you'd hit my sister, Elsa, this would be . . ." She paused for a moment. "Yeesh! Because, you know . . ." Anna patted the horse, trying to recover her rambling thoughts. "Hello," she said to the horse. She turned back to Hans and offered him a princess grin. "But lucky for you, it's just me."

"Just you?" Hans asked. A warm smile spread across his face.

Anna couldn't help smiling back. All of sudden, the castle bells began to peal.

"The bells!" she cried. "The coronation—I'd better go," she said. She hopped off the boat onto the pier and waved. "Uh, bye!"

Hans waved back. Even the horse waved, lifting his hoof off the boat for a moment. Unfortunately, that caused the boat's weight to shift again.

"Oh, no!" Hans said.

The boat flipped off the dock and Hans fell into the water with a splash! Lifting the boat off his head, Hans peeked up from the water and watched Anna run through the streets toward the castle. He grinned as he thought about his wonderful chance meeting with the beautiful princess.

··❥⊃·⊙≻ —— ❀· —— ⧁·⧀⧀··

Soon the people of Arendelle, along with dignitaries from around the land, were making their way into the royal church for Elsa's coronation. Kristoff, however, was far away, in a corner of the town. He had sold all his ice and was now busy bargaining for a brand-new sled.

"Watch this, Sven," Kristoff called as he played

around with the sled's special features, which allowed it to switch between runners and wheels. "It's a sled! It's a wagon! It's a sled! It's a wagon!"

The sled salesman looked concerned, as if he was wondering what kind of person would talk to a reindeer. But he wanted to finish the sale. He tried to make small talk as they completed their deal. "You sticking around to see the queen and the princess?" he asked Kristoff.

"Are you kidding?" Kristoff replied. "I've got a brand-new sled . . . with wheels!" He grinned. "I'm hitting the road."

"Suit yourself," the man said. "But I bet they're beautiful."

Kristoff didn't even hear the man. He and Sven were already headed back to the mountains with their new sled.

6

The cathedral was packed with people as the coronation ceremony began. An orchestra played and a choir sang while the royal procession walked down the very long center aisle. The bishop led the way, followed by Elsa, looking regal and serious, and finally Anna, holding the train of Elsa's dress.

At the altar, Elsa and Anna faced the bishop. Near him lay a silver platter holding the royal crown, scepter, and orb.

Peeking over her shoulder, Anna spotted the handsome Prince Hans. He sat straight and tall, and a stranger was asleep on his shoulder! Hans waved at Anna, who giggled.

The bishop placed the crown on Elsa's head. Then he turned for the scepter and orb and presented them to Elsa. She reached for the royal items, but the bishop cleared his throat. "Ahem. Your gloves, Your Majesty."

Elsa took a sharp breath. If she took the gloves off, she might accidentally let out her icy magic. She hesitated, growing pale with worry.

Anna took that moment to look over at Hans and smile at him. She couldn't wait to talk to him at the ball!

Elsa slowly removed her gloves and placed them on the satin pillow. With a deep breath, she took the orb and scepter into her hands. She turned to face the crowd.

"As the undoubted queen, protector of this dominion," the bishop intoned, "keeper of the doctrine and government thereof from this day forward, I present to you Her Majesty . . ."

Elsa's eyes widened as the scepter and orb began to freeze in her hands! She tried desperately to control her emotions. She was just so nervous!

". . . Queen Elsa of Arendelle!" The bishop finished his decree.

The people in the church rose. "Queen Elsa of Arendelle!" they echoed.

Elsa quickly placed the orb and scepter back on

the silver tray and grabbed her gloves. With a sigh of relief, she realized that no one had seen the ice on the orb or the scepter. She smiled at the cheering crowd. She had made it through the ceremony!

Later, at the coronation ball, Elsa and Anna stood side by side in a long receiving line at the entrance to the Great Hall. Elsa felt relaxed, almost content, now that the most difficult part of Coronation Day was over. Festive music filled the air as guests danced across the floor of the lavishly decorated ballroom.

"You look beautiful," Elsa said to Anna.

"Thank you," Anna said in surprise. A smile spread across her face. Her sister had actually spoken to her! "You look beautiful-er," Anna replied. Then she realized how strange that had sounded and blurted out an explanation. "Not that you're fuller. No. Just more beautiful!"

Elsa grinned. "Thank you." Then she looked out at the crowded ballroom. "So this is what a party looks like?"

Anna nodded. "It's warmer than I thought."

"All the people, I guess," Elsa said. "And what is that amazing smell?"

Both of them caught a whiff of a sweet aroma wafting across the room. "Chocolate!" they exclaimed at the same time. Then they looked at each other and started laughing.

Anna could hardly believe that Elsa was treating her so kindly. She was about to say more to her sister, but just then, a guest stepped up to be presented to the new queen and the princess. "The Duke of Weaseltown," a royal attendant announced.

"Weselton," the Duke corrected him. Then he bowed his head. "As your closest partner in trade, it seems only fitting that I offer you your first dance as queen."

Elsa stiffened and clasped her gloved hands together. "Thank you," she said. "But I don't dance."

The Duke looked offended, so Elsa quickly nudged Anna forward. "But my sister is a marvelous dancer."

Anna was a little startled, but she allowed the Duke to lead her to the dance floor.

Unfortunately, the Duke was a horrible dancer. He couldn't seem to take one step without crushing Anna's toes. As he bobbed up and down, his toupee bounced back and forth on his head—and he never stopped talking.

"Bump-be-dump-bah! Look at me!" he crowed. "This certainly makes up for being shut out for twelve years for no reason. Do you know the reason?" he asked Anna. "No? Well, watch this: like a chicken with the face of a monkey, I fly!"

Anna cringed as the Duke danced around her like a dying peacock. Then she caught sight of Elsa watching from the side of the room, barely able to keep from laughing. Anna shot Elsa a number of "help me" looks, but there was no way out of it. She was forced to finish the dance, much to Elsa's amusement.

After the dance, Anna limped back to Elsa. "Well, he was sprightly," said the queen with a smile.

"Especially for a man in heels!" Anna replied. Both sisters giggled.

"Are you all right?" Elsa asked more gently.

Anna smiled. "I've never been better," she said, glancing into Elsa's eyes. "This is so nice. I wish it could be like this all the time."

"Me too," Elsa said wistfully. Then she caught herself and stiffened. "But it can't."

"Why not?" Anna asked, surprised at Elsa's sudden change of attitude.

Elsa tensed. "Because it can't," she said firmly.

Anna felt all her old disappointment rushing back. "Excuse me," she said. Elsa watched sadly as Anna walked away.

7

$\mathcal{A}$nna pushed through the crowd of guests, and one of the dancers tripped into her, knocking her backward. Someone grabbed her by the arms before she hit the floor.

"Glad I caught you," Hans said, smiling.

"Hans!" she said, surprised.

Hans lifted Anna back to her feet, and the two immediately were drawn into the dance. Hans was an excellent dancer, and Anna was happy to let him guide her around the ballroom, twirling her at just the right moments. She was amazed at how natural it felt.

After that, she and Hans walked and laughed and danced some more. One hour turned into many hours of them talking and enjoying each other's company.

Finally, they took a break and strolled into the rose

garden. Hans plucked a rose and placed it in Anna's hair. As he did, he noticed the white streak running down the side of her head. "What's this?"

Anna put her hand to her hair. "I was born with it," she told him. "Although I dreamt I was kissed by a troll."

"I like it," Hans said.

On the balcony, they sat on a bench and Anna taught Hans how to eat a krumkake. "Just bite it. The whole thing!" she said. The pair laughed as the treat crumbled all over Hans's face.

Hans told Anna about his family. "I have twelve older brothers," he said. "Three of them pretended I was invisible . . . for two years."

"That's horrible," Anna said.

"It's what brothers do," he replied with a shrug.

Anna smiled knowingly. "And sisters," she added. "Elsa and I were really close when we were little. But then one day she just shut me out, and I never knew why."

"I would never shut you out," Hans said, gazing into Anna's eyes.

Anna beamed. "Okay, can I just say something crazy?" she asked.

"I love crazy," Hans said with a wide grin.

"All my life has been a series of doors in my face," she said. "Then suddenly, I bump into you!" Anna explained that she felt like she'd been waiting her whole life to meet him. And Hans agreed. He felt the same way! Anna couldn't believe her good fortune. At last, here was someone who understood her. Someone who was open to new experiences and people, exactly the way she was. Hans was sweet, kind, and fun. They spent the rest of the party together, dancing, laughing, and discussing their pasts—and their futures, too.

"Can I say something crazy?" Hans asked suddenly. "Will you marry me?"

Anna gasped. "Can I just—ooh. I mean, yes!" She was amazed that she and Hans had found each other. She just knew that they were meant to be.

"Elsa!" Anna called from across the ballroom. She pulled Hans toward her sister. "May I present Prince Hans of the Southern Isles," she said formally.

"Your Majesty." Hans greeted the queen with a deep bow.

Anna was beaming. "We would like—"

"—your blessing—" Hans continued.

"—of our marriage!" Anna finished breathlessly.

"Marriage?" Elsa asked. "I'm confused."

"Well, we haven't worked out all the details," Anna said. "We'll need a few days to plan the ceremony. Of course, we'll have soup, roast, and ice cream . . ." Anna turned to Hans. "Would we live here?"

"Here?" Elsa asked.

"Absolutely!" Hans cried.

"What? No," Elsa said.

"And we'll invite all twelve of your brothers to stay here with us, and—" Anna stopped as Elsa put up her hand.

"Wait," she said. "Slow down. Anna, no one's brothers are staying here. No one is getting married."

Anna's mouth dropped open. "Wait, what?"

"I need to talk to you," Elsa said sternly. "Alone."

Anna linked her arm with Hans's. "No," she said. "Whatever you have to say, you can say to both of us."

Elsa shook her head. "No. . . . You can't marry a man you just met."

Standing straighter, Anna spoke up. "You can if it's true love."

"What do you know about true love?" Elsa replied, scoffing at her sister's naiveté.

"More than you," Anna replied. "All you want is to be alone."

Elsa took a deep breath. "You asked for my blessing, but my answer is no. Now, if you'll excuse me," she said, and started to move away.

"Your Majesty," Hans said. "If I may—"

"No, you may not," Elsa snapped. "And I think you should go." She walked off and signaled to one of the guards. "The party is over. It's time to close the gates."

Anna ran after her. "Elsa! No!" She reached for her sister and grabbed her hand. As she tugged at her to stay, Elsa's glove slipped off.

"Give me my glove!" Elsa exclaimed.

Anna held the glove up and away from Elsa. "No, listen to me," she said, "I can't live like this anymore!"

Elsa fought to gain control. "Then leave," she finally said. She saw the hurt on Anna's face. She turned to flee from the room.

"What did I ever do to you?" Anna cried.

"Enough, Anna!" Elsa ordered.

"Why do you shut me out?" Anna asked. "Why do you shut the world out? What are you so afraid of?"

"I said enough!" Elsa shouted, spinning around.

As she did, ice shot from her bare hand, coating the floor of the ballroom and frothing up into icy plumes.

The music stopped abruptly and everyone turned to stare at Elsa in shock. She stared at her subjects, wishing with all her heart that she could take the magic back.

But it was too late. Sheets of ice covered the dance floor. The Great Hall fell into a chilly silence.

The Duke gasped. "Sorcery! I knew there was something going on here."

"Elsa?" Anna called, but Elsa was already pushing through the doors and racing out of the room.

8

Elsa burst into the courtyard. She was so afraid now that her secret was out. She hoped she hadn't hurt anyone. Regardless, everyone in Arendelle would soon know about her magic.

"There she is!" cried a townswoman, excited to get a glimpse of the newly crowned queen. The woman obviously had no idea what had just happened in the ballroom. "Your Majesty! Long live the queen! Queen Elsa!"

Elsa backed away from the woman and quickly weaved through the crowd, trying hard not to touch anyone as she backed away. She didn't want to cause any harm with her powers. She just wanted to leave the kingdom and hide!

A young woman with a small child in her arms called to her. "Your Majesty, are you all right?" she asked, full of concern.

Elsa put her hands behind her and moved away. She slowly walked backward, accidentally bumping into the fountain in the center of the courtyard. As soon as she touched the fountain, the water in it froze to solid ice.

There was a loud gasp from the villagers. People turned and ran away from Elsa.

The Duke and his guards ran down the castle steps. "There she is!" he shouted, leading the charge toward Elsa. "Get her!"

"Just stay away from me! Stay away!" Elsa cried. She held her hands up, causing the castle steps to ice over. The Duke's guards slipped and tumbled down to the ground.

"Monster!" the Duke hissed.

The crowd panicked. A swirl of cold air traveled through Arendelle as Elsa ran along the streets, leaving ice and snow in her wake.

Anna watched from the castle gates. "Elsa!" she called. "Wait, please!" She rushed from the castle and ran after Elsa. Hans trailed behind her. "Elsa!" Anna cried desperately.

Elsa looked over her shoulder as she neared the water. When she turned, her foot touched the lapping waves—and the water in the fjord immediately froze. She took another cautious step . . . and another sheet of ice bloomed under her foot.

"Elsa!" Anna called after her.

Feeling her panic grow, Elsa ran across the fjord. With each step, more water froze underneath her. Soon she was moving at full speed, heading toward the mountains on the other side of the lake. As she passed, the ships belonging to the visiting dignitaries creaked and locked into place, frozen in the ice. The gorgeous summer day had turned into a growing winter storm.

"Elsa, stop!" Anna pleaded. She rushed onto the fjord after her sister but slipped on the ice. She was too far behind to catch up.

Hans reached out for Anna and helped her to stand. "Anna, are you all right?" he asked.

They both watched as Elsa reached the far shore and made her way into the mountains. Anna strained to see the path Elsa had taken.

"Did you know?" Hans asked Anna.

"No," Anna replied. Then she nodded. "But it makes so much sense."

They walked back through the village and overheard the Duke speaking. He was addressing a growing crowd of concerned people. "The queen has cursed this land," he said. "She must be stopped! You must go after her!"

Anna rushed over to him. "No!" she shouted. "No one is to go anywhere."

"You!" The Duke shook a finger at Anna. "Is there sorcery in you, too?" he shouted. "Are you a monster, too?"

"No, I'm completely ordinary," Anna replied.

Hans took her hand. "That's right, she is," he told the Duke.

"And my sister is not a monster," Anna added.

The Duke scowled. "She nearly killed me," he said dramatically.

"You slipped on ice," Hans pointed out.

Anna stepped forward. "It was an accident. She was scared. She didn't mean it. She didn't mean any of this." She paused. "All she's ever wanted is to be perfect and good. Tonight was my fault. I pushed her. So I'm the one who needs to go after her."

Anna turned to her royal guards. "Bring me my horse, please."

"What? Anna, no!" Hans shouted. "It's too dangerous."

"I'm not afraid of Elsa," Anna said. "I'll bring her back and make this right."

A royal guard brought Anna's horse to her. She took her cloak, which was hanging over the saddle, and wrapped it around her shoulders.

"I'm coming with you," Hans said.

"No," Anna told him. "I need you here to take care of Arendelle."

Hans saw the desperation in Anna's eyes. He put his hand to his chest. "On my honor," he said, bowing his head.

"I leave Prince Hans in charge!" Anna told the crowd.

"Are you sure you can trust her?" Hans asked as Anna mounted the horse. When Anna didn't reply, he leaned in. "I don't want you getting hurt."

"She's my sister," Anna said. "She'd never hurt me."

Urging her horse into a gallop, Anna took off over the frozen fjord toward the mountains as snow continued to fall.

··»⟩·›»———❀———«‹·«⟨··

Elsa trudged up the steep North Mountain. Ever since she was a child, she had been taught to conceal her powers. Now that was all over. She felt sad and worried as she gazed back at Arendelle far below. She knew no one in Arendelle would ever see her in the same way again.

But a tiny part of her also felt relieved. Her magic had been a hard secret to keep, and she didn't have to hide it anymore. Being alone was easier, too. She didn't have to worry about hurting anyone.

As she continued up the mountain, her steps actually became a little lighter. Now that everyone knew what she was capable of, she was free to be herself!

With a wave of her hand, Elsa started to experiment with her magic. Snow and ice whirled around her as she created snowmen and icy patterns in the air. The farther she got from Arendelle, the more confident she felt. As she took each step, her ability to draw forth ice and cold grew stronger and more powerful.

Elsa plucked off her crown and threw it aside. She tossed her head and her tightly bound hair came loose, cascading over one shoulder in a thick, wavy braid. Twirling around, she conjured up a flowing new outfit of ice, a crystal-blue gown with a cape of gossamer frost. Snow was her element. She was the Snow Queen!

Thrilled to let her powers loose at last, Elsa found that she could do more than she realized. As she released her magic, a staircase of ice extended upward . . . to an exquisite ice palace that grew as she raised her arms!

This was where she would live. When the castle was finished, Elsa slammed the door. She was home at last.

9

$\mathcal{T}$he wind howled and the snow blew into Anna's face. She struggled to guide her horse up the frozen mountain path. She was determined to find Elsa. Anna was sure her sister would thaw the fjord and bring back summer. The whole kingdom would celebrate, and the two sisters would live happily ever after. The thought encouraged Anna as she rode through the snowdrifts.

"Elsa!" Anna called into the blizzard. "It's me, Anna. Your sister who didn't mean to make you freeze the summer!" She paused, shivering in the cold. "Wow, that's a sentence I never thought I'd say. Anyway, I'm sorry! This is all my f-f-f-fault."

A wolf's howl interrupted Anna's cries.

Her horse stopped and looked around nervously. Anna tried to convince herself that the sounds were just puppies playing.

"Of course, none of this would have happened if she'd just told me her secret," Anna said with a sigh.

A tree branch snapped, and the horse panicked. It whinnied and kicked up its front legs.

"Whoa, whoa!" Anna commanded, pulling back on the reins. She flew off the horse into a snowdrift! She sat up, spit snow out of her mouth, and looked around just in time to see her horse running away.

"No, no, no! Come back!" Anna called, but the horse was long gone. "Okay," she said to herself. She had to keep focused. She struggled to stand up and dusted the snow off her dress.

"Snow, it had to be snow," she grumbled. "She couldn't have had a tropical magic that covered the fjords in white sand and warm . . ." A welcome sight interrupted Anna's rant. She saw smoke rising in the distance. "Fire!"

Anna took one more step and stumbled down a steep hill. She began to roll like a snowball, layering on more and more snow as she went.

Anna landed with a splash in an icy stream and the snowball broke apart. She got to her feet, shivering. "Cold, cold, cold, cold, cold . . . ," she muttered. She was standing next to a small building. A wooden sign hung in front of her: WANDERING OAKEN'S TRADING POST. A lump of snow fell off the sign. "And sauna!" she said, reading the end of the sign.

Anna hurried inside. The little shop was stocked with summer supplies—after all, it was technically still summertime. She gazed at the goods, looking for warm clothes.

"Hoo, hoo!" called a blond man behind the counter wearing a bright sweater. His name was Oaken, and he was the owner. "Big summer blowout," he said hopefully. "Half off on our swimming suits, clogs, and a sun balm of my own invention, *ja?*"

"Oh, great," Anna said, looking around the store. "For now, how about boots? Winter boots and dresses?"

"Well, that would be in our winter department," the man said in a thick accent.

Anna darted toward the single rack of warm clothing. "Oh, um, I was just wondering," she said, trying to sound casual, "has another young woman, the queen, perhaps, I don't know, passed through here?" She brought a pair of boots and some clothes to the counter and set them in front of Oaken.

"Only one crazy enough to be out in the storm is

you, dear," Oaken said in a pleasant voice.

At that moment, the front door opened and a gust of frigid air blew in. A large, broad man entered. He was dressed for the arctic cold and completely covered in snow, with only his brown eyes showing. It was Kristoff, and he was looking for supplies, too.

"You and this fellow. Hoo, hoo," Oaken sang out. "Big summer blowout."

Kristoff pushed past Oaken and went straight to Anna. "Carrots," he demanded.

"Huh?" Anna asked.

"Behind you," Kristoff said crossly, pointing.

"Oh, right," Anna said. "Excuse me." She moved out of the way, and Kristoff grabbed a bag of carrots from a shelf behind her. He gathered a few other supplies as he moved briskly around the shop.

"A real howler in July, *ja?*" Oaken said, trying to make conversation with the stranger. "Wherever could it be coming from?"

"The North Mountain," Kristoff replied.

"The North Mountain," Anna repeated to herself. Was that where Elsa had gone?

10

*K*ristoff brought his pile of supplies to the front counter.

"That'll be forty, *ja?*" Oaken said.

"Forty?" Kristoff barked. "No, ten."

"No, see, these are from our winter stock," Oaken told him. "Where supply and demand have a big problem."

"You want to talk about a supply-and-demand problem?" Kristoff asked. "I sell ice for a living!"

Anna walked over to the counter and smiled at Kristoff. "Ice. Really?" she said. "That's a rough business to be in right now."

"Forty," Oaken repeated. "But I will throw in a visit to Oaken's sauna. Hoo, hoo!"

Kristoff and Anna both peered over Oaken's shoulder to see a family waving from a toasty sauna in a room behind him.

"Ten's all I got," Kristoff told him. "Help me out, *ja?*"

Oaken held up the bag of carrots. "Ten will get you this and no more."

Kristoff glared at Oaken, seething.

"Just tell me one thing," Anna said, moving closer to Kristoff. "What was happening on the North Mountain? Did it seem . . . magical?"

Kristoff pulled down his scarf, revealing his face. He looked down sharply at Anna. "Yes!" he shouted. "Now back up while I deal with this crook here."

Oaken rose from his chair. He did not appreciate being called a crook. "What did you call me?" he said. He was much taller and wider than Kristoff had expected. Oaken loomed over the counter. Then, with a frown, Oaken swiftly threw Kristoff out of the shop.

Kristoff went flying out the door and landed face-first in a mound of snow next to Sven, who had been waiting patiently outside. Kristoff pulled his head out of the snow. "Ow!" he moaned.

"Goodbye!" Oaken said pleasantly, and slammed the door.

The reindeer snorted and moved over to Kristoff,

snuffling and searching in the snow.

"No, Sven," Kristoff told him. "I didn't get your carrots."

The hungry reindeer huffed in his face. Then Kristoff turned his head and spotted something that made him brighten. There was a barn behind the trading post—a warm place to spend the night.

"But I did find us a place to sleep," he added. "And it's free."

Back in the shop, Oaken returned to his other customer. "I'm sorry about this violence," he told Anna. "I will add a quart of lutefisk so we have good feelings." He looked over at what she had selected. "Just the outfit and the boots, *ja?*"

Anna looked at her supplies, and then over at the bag Kristoff had left on the counter. She smiled as an idea occurred to her.

Shortly afterward, Anna left Oaken's shop and looked around. She could hear singing coming from the barn. She pushed open the door quietly and peered inside. Kristoff was lying against a bale of hay, playing his lute. He was singing to his reindeer . . . and then, singing as Sven, he finished the song from the reindeer's point of view.

"Ahem." Anna cleared her throat. When Kristoff looked over, she smiled. "Nice duet," she said.

"Oh, it's just you," he said when he saw Anna standing in front of him. "What do you want?"

"I want you to take me up the North Mountain," she declared.

"I don't take people places," Kristoff replied. He closed his eyes and lay back in the hay.

"Let me rephrase that," Anna said. She threw the sack of supplies she had just bought over to Kristoff. They were exactly the items he'd wanted.

"Umph!" he grunted as the heavy bag landed on his chest.

"Take me up the North Mountain," she ordered.

Kristoff regarded her carefully. He was not used to taking orders. And he especially couldn't see any reason to follow Anna's.

"Look," Anna said. "I know how to stop this winter."

Kristoff hesitated. If the cold weather stopped, he might be able to sell his ice down in Arendelle again.

"We leave at dawn," he said finally. "And you forgot the carrots for Sven."

Anna dropped a bag of carrots on Kristoff's face.

"Ooh!" he said.

"Oops, sorry, sorry," Anna said. Then she caught herself. She was trying to take charge, after all. "We leave now," she declared. "Right now!"

Kristoff looked over at Sven and offered him a carrot. Sven took a healthy bite. So did Kristoff. They looked at the stranger before them as they chewed. They both knew she had no clue what was ahead.

11

Kristoff held the reins tightly, steering Sven and the sled through the thick, heavy snow. The night sky was cloudy with the promise of still more snow.

"Hang on!" Kristoff yelled to his passenger. "We like to go fast!"

Sven responded happily and charged forward through the drifts.

"I like fast," Anna answered. She leaned back and put her feet up on the front of the sled to show that she was not bothered by the high speed.

"Get your feet down," Kristoff scoffed. "This is fresh lacquer." He glanced at her sideways. "Seriously, were you raised in a barn?" He leaned over and wiped down his new sled.

"No, I was raised in a castle," Anna replied.

"So tell me," Kristoff said, "what made the queen go all ice crazy?"

"It was all my fault," Anna blurted out. "I got engaged and she freaked out, because I'd only just met him, you know, that day. And she said she wouldn't bless the marriage."

"Wait," Kristoff said. "You got engaged to someone you just met that day?"

"Yeah, anyway," Anna replied, dismissing his comment. "I got mad and yelled at her, and she tried to walk away, but I grabbed her glove, and—"

"Wait. You got engaged to someone you just met that day?" Kristoff repeated.

"Yes, are you listening?" Anna snapped. "Thing is, she wore the gloves all the time, but I just thought the girl's got a thing about dirt."

"Didn't your parents ever warn you about strangers?" Kristoff asked.

"Yes, they did," Anna said. She looked Kristoff over carefully and slid farther away from him on the seat. After all, he was a stranger. "But Hans is not a stranger."

Kristoff raised his eyebrows. "Oh, yeah? What's his last name?"

Anna frowned, thinking. "Of the Southern Isles?" she offered.

"What's his favorite food?" Kristoff fired off.

Anna hesitated. "Sandwiches."

"Best friend's name?" Kristoff quickly followed up.

"Probably John," Anna replied, reflecting that lots of people were named John. So maybe Hans's best friend would be, too.

"Eye color?" Kristoff pressed.

"Dreamy." Anna smiled.

"Have you had a meal with him yet?" Kristoff asked. "What if you hate the way he eats? What if you hate the way he picks his nose?"

Anna wrinkled her forehead. "Picks his nose?"

"And eats it," Kristoff added.

"Excuse me, sir," Anna said. "He is a prince."

Kristoff shook his head. "All men do it."

"Ewww!" Anna made a face. "Look, it doesn't matter. It's true love."

"Doesn't sound like true love," Kristoff said, staring straight ahead.

"Are you some sort of love expert?" Anna asked.

"No, but I have friends who are," he responded.

"You have friends who are love experts?" Anna asked sarcastically.

Kristoff's eyes widened and he stopped the sled. "Stop talking," he demanded.

"No, I want to meet these friends," she insisted with a grin.

Kristoff put his hand over Anna's mouth. "I mean it. Shhhh!" He stood up and looked into the dark woods. He held up a lantern. Suddenly, he yelled, "Sven! Go! GO!"

The sled took off and Anna fell backward. She saw glowing eyes in the darkness all around them. "What are they?" she whispered.

"Wolves," Kristoff said.

"What do we do?" Anna asked. She looked at Kristoff and readied herself.

"I've got this," Kristoff said calmly. "You just don't fall off—and don't get eaten."

"But I want to help," Anna said.

"No," Kristoff replied.

"Why not?" Anna pouted.

"Because I don't trust your judgment," Kristoff said.

Anna was offended. "Excuse me?"

A wolf jumped at the sleigh, and Kristoff kicked it back. "Who marries a man she's just met?"

Anna was seething. "It's true love!" She picked up Kristoff's lute and swung it at his head. He ducked, and Anna struck a wolf that was about to lunge onto the sled!

"Whoa!" Kristoff exclaimed, just as another wolf jumped up and knocked him down. He fell out and was dragged behind the sled.

"Christopher!" Anna cried.

"It's Kristoff!" he yelled.

Anna took the lantern and lit the sled's blanket on fire. She threw the flaming blanket toward Kristoff, and the wolves tumbled off him. Then she reached out and pulled him back onto the sled. Kristoff looked at her in dismay.

"You almost set me on fire," he said.

"But I didn't," Anna replied.

Sven suddenly whinnied. Ahead of him was a steep drop into a massive gorge.

"Get ready to jump, Sven!" Anna called.

"You don't tell him what to do!" Kristoff shouted. "I do!"

In one swift movement, he grabbed Anna and threw her onto Sven's back. Then he unhooked the reindeer's harness. "Jump!"

Sven leaped and cleared the gorge with Anna on his back.

Just behind them, Kristoff boldly jumped with the sled. The sled didn't make it all the way across, but just before it fell into the gorge, Kristoff threw himself off and caught the edge of the cliff on the other side. Down below, his new sled burst into flames as he dangled from the cliff. "I just got it." He looked down with a sigh. Then his hands started to slip on the slick ice. "Uh-oh," he said in alarm. "No, no, no!"

Out of nowhere, an ax slammed into the snow just inches from his face. He heard Anna's voice from above.

"Grab on!" she yelled.

The ax was attached to a rope that was secured around Sven.

"Pull, Sven!" Anna ordered.

Sven heaved and walked backward, lifting Kristoff to safety.

Anna and Kristoff peered over the edge at the burning sled. "I'll replace your sled and everything in it," she promised. She looked sadly at Kristoff. "And I understand if you don't want to help me anymore."

Kristoff watched as Anna walked away. Sven nuzzled him softly with his cold nose.

"Of course I don't want to help her anymore," he told the reindeer. "In fact, this whole thing has ruined me for helping anyone ever again." He watched as Anna turned and started to walk in the opposite direction.

"But she'll die on her own," he said, speaking in Sven's deep voice.

Kristoff looked away. "I can live with that," he said.

Anna turned this way and that, unsure which way to go.

"But you won't get your new sled if she's dead," Kristoff continued in Sven's voice.

He sighed. "Wait up," he called to Anna in his normal voice. "We're coming."

Anna grinned. "You are?" she said happily. Then she composed herself. "I mean, sure, I'll let you tag along."

Anna wasn't sure what lay ahead, but she was very glad that Kristoff and Sven were coming with her.

12

Together, Kristoff, Sven, and Anna walked through the night. As dawn crept over the horizon, the three travelers found themselves on the rim of a mountain. Looking down, they could see Arendelle in the distance.

But it wasn't the summertime view they were expecting. The kingdom was completely frozen, covered with white ice.

Anna gasped in shock. Then she pulled herself together. "It'll be fine," she said. "Elsa will thaw it."

"Will she?" Kristoff asked skeptically. "Just like that?"

"Sure," Anna replied. She pointed straight ahead. "Come on. This way to the North Mountain, right?"

"More like this way," Kristoff said, pushing her pointing finger upward. A huge, steep mountain towered above them.

The young royals, Elsa and Anna, have great fun together, especially when Elsa shows off her magical ice powers. It's the sisters' secret.

Elsa accidentally hurts Anna, but a wise troll knows how to save her little sister.

Elsa loves her sister and doesn't want to hurt her again.

Anna misses Elsa, who stays away from her. She does not know that Elsa is doing it to protect her.

Years later, Anna wakes up overjoyed. It's her sister's
coronation day! Elsa will become Queen of Arendelle.

Anna meets a visiting prince named Hans.

Anna is smitten with the dashing—and handsome—Hans.

Now that Elsa is queen, Anna hopes she will get to spend
more time with her.

Anna dances the night away with Hans.
She thinks she is in love.

Hans proposes to Anna, and she says yes—even though she
has only known him for one day!

The sisters argue. Angry and upset, Elsa accidentally reveals her magical powers to the whole kingdom.

Elsa runs away. She lets her powers surge like a storm.

Elsa has never felt so free. She creates a kingdom
of ice and snow for herself.

Arendelle becomes locked in an eternal winter!

Anna sets out alone to find her sister.

A rugged mountain man named Kristoff and his reindeer, Sven, agree to help Anna.

Near Elsa's ice palace, they meet a funny living
snowman named Olaf.

Even though he is a snowman, Olaf dreams
of enjoying a warm summer day.

Olaf seems familiar. Anna has forgotten that she and Elsa
built a snowman named Olaf when they were children.

Hans sets out to find of Anna—and to stop Elsa if she refuses
to free Arendelle.

Anna finally finds Elsa, but Elsa is happy being alone
in her ice palace.

Elsa accidentally hits Anna in the heart with a bolt of ice.
Horrified, Elsa begs Anna to leave.

Elsa creates a snow giant to chase Anna and Kristoff away.
Olaf names him Marshmallow!

"Don't come back!" Marshmallow growls.
Anna and Kristoff run!

As Anna freezes, she tries to stay warm in the castle. She does not know that Hans is not the good man she thinks he is.

Olaf tries to help Anna. She desperately wants to find Elsa.

Hans lies and tells Elsa that Anna has died. Elsa is heartbroken.

Anna goes in search of Elsa.

Anna's act of true love saved Elsa—and Anna, too!
The sisters hug with joy.

Elsa gives Olaf his own snow cloud to keep him cold
wherever he goes. Now he can finally enjoy summer!

Anna and Kristoff know they belong together.
They share their first kiss!

Arendelle is once again a warm and happy kingdom—
and Elsa and Anna are the happiest of all!

With no other choice, the group continued, moving forward and up. As the sun finally rose completely, they rounded a corner and came upon a clearing surrounded by tall trees.

They gasped as the morning light danced on the snowy area before them. The terrain was different from what they had seen in the rest of the woods. They had found a gorgeous winter wonderland.

The view took Anna's breath away. "I never knew winter could be so . . . beautiful," she said, looking up at a willow tree covered in ice. The branches looked as if they were glistening with a crystal coating. Then she noticed Sven. The reindeer had gotten his antlers tangled up in icy vines, and he looked like a twinkling Christmas tree!

"Yeah, but it's so white!" said a voice that came out of nowhere. "Does it hurt your eyes? My eyes are killing me. You know, how about a little color?"

Anna and Kristoff looked around. They stared at Sven for a moment. Could he be the one speaking?

"Must we bleach the joy out of it all?" the voice went on. "I'm thinking like maybe some crimson or chartreuse. How about yellow? No, not yellow. Yellow and snow? Brrrr . . . No go."

A goofy little snowman with twigs for arms, but no nose, appeared. He laughed at his own yellow snow joke. "Am I right?" he asked Anna.

"AAAAHHH!" Anna screamed. She'd never seen a talking snowman before, and she reacted quickly. She kicked him in the snowball head, which went flying right into Kristoff.

"Hi!" the snowman head said.

"You're creepy," Kristoff told the head. He tossed it to Anna.

"I don't want it!" Anna shrieked, throwing it back to Kristoff.

"Back at you!" Kristoff called, chucking the head to her again.

"Please don't drop me!" the snowman head pleaded.

Anna frowned at Kristoff. "Don't!"

Kristoff grinned. "Come on, it's just a head," he said.

"All right," the snowman told them. "We got off to a bad start."

"The body!" Anna cried. She quickly dropped the head onto the body, but somehow it landed upside down—and stuck that way.

"Wait!" the snowman said, gazing at the upside-down world around him. "What am I looking at right now? Why are you hanging off the earth like a bat?"

Anna walked over to the snowman. "All right," she said. "Wait one second." She turned his head around so he was right-side up.

"Oh, thank you!" he said.

"You're welcome," Anna said, smiling at the little snowman. He wasn't so scary now that she'd gotten a chance to look at him properly.

"Now I'm perfect," the snowman said.

"Well, almost," Anna replied. She grabbed a carrot from Sven's pack and pushed it into Olaf's face to give him a nose. She pushed a little too forcefully, though, and the carrot went right through his head! "Oh, too hard!" Anna said. "I'm sorry! I— I was just . . ."

The snowman spun around. "Woo!" he exclaimed. "Head rush!"

Anna bent down to him. "Are you okay?"

He beamed. Even though only a tiny point of the carrot was sticking out in front, he was happy. "Are you kidding me?" he asked. "I am wonderful! I've always wanted a nose." He looked down, cross-eyed, at his new feature. "So cute. It's like a little baby unicorn."

With another shove, Anna pushed the carrot from the back of his head so the carrot nose was in the proper place.

"What? Hey! Whoa!" the snowman cried out. "I love it even more! All right, let's start this thing over." A smile spread across his face. "Hi, everyone! I'm Olaf, and I like warm hugs." He opened his twig arms wide for a hug.

The name struck Anna. "Olaf?" she asked. Anna thought for a moment. She remembered building a little snowman with Elsa when they were young. Elsa had given that snowman the same name.

Olaf gazed at Anna. "And you are?"

"I'm Anna," she answered.

"And who is the funky-looking donkey over there?" Olaf inquired.

"That's Sven," Anna told him.

"Uh-huh," Olaf said. "And who's the reindeer?"

"Sven!" Anna said, laughing at Olaf's mistake.

Confused, Olaf stared at both Sven and Kristoff, thinking they had the same name. "Oh, okay. Makes things easier for me," he said.

Sven moved closer to the talking snowman and tried to take a bite of Olaf's carrot nose.

"Aww," Olaf said, laughing. "Look at him, trying to kiss my nose." He smiled at the reindeer. "I like you, too!"

"Olaf, did Elsa build you?" Anna asked.

"Yeah, why?" the snowman replied.

"Do you know where she is?" Anna said, moving closer.

"Yeah, why?" Olaf said, innocently oblivious to the line of questioning.

"Do you think you could show us the way?" Anna asked, full of hope.

"Yeah, why?" the snowman asked again.

Kristoff was busy examining one of Olaf's twig arms, which had fallen off. "How does this work?"

The hand on the arm smacked Kristoff across the face!

"Stop it, Sven!" Olaf said, calling Kristoff by the wrong name. "We need to focus here!" He turned to face Anna. "Why?"

"I'll tell you why," Kristoff said. "We need Elsa to bring back summer."

"Summer?" Olaf said. "Oh, I don't know why, but

I've always loved the idea of summer and sun, and all things hot!"

Kristoff raised his eyebrows. "Really? I'm guessing you don't have much experience with heat."

Olaf shook his head. "Nope, but sometimes I like to close my eyes and imagine what it'd be like when summer does come."

As Olaf went on and on about all the wonderful things he would do in summer, Kristoff looked over at Anna. "I'm going to tell him," he whispered. It was killing him to hear Olaf talk about summer's heat—which is a snowman's worst nightmare!

"Don't you dare," Anna scolded Kristoff. She couldn't bear to ruin Olaf's dream with the harsh truth.

Olaf took Anna's hand. "So come on! Let's go bring back summer!"

"I'm coming!" Anna said. She looked over her shoulder at Kristoff.

"Somebody's got to tell him," Kristoff murmured, shaking his head. He and Sven followed Anna and the little snowman.

13

*A*nna, Kristoff, and Sven followed Olaf through a maze of icicles, hoping to find Elsa. But it looked as if whoever had built the path did not want visitors. Sharp ice daggers stuck out of the ground everywhere. Kristoff just missed being jabbed in the chest by one of the thick spikes.

"So how exactly are you planning to stop this weather?" he asked Anna.

"I'm going to talk to my sister," she said.

"That's your plan?" Kristoff replied. "My whole business is riding on you talking to your sister?"

Anna marched forward. "Yep."

"And you're not at all afraid of her?" Kristoff asked.

"Why would I be?" Anna said.

Kristoff peered at the sharp ice spikes lining the path.

"I was just literally thinking the same thing," Olaf

said. "I bet Elsa's the nicest, gentlest, warmest person ever." He walked right into an icicle that pierced his torso. His bottom section continued to walk forward into a snow mound. When Olaf realized his body was no longer connected, he began to laugh. "Oh, look at that," he said. "I've been impaled."

Anna and Kristoff didn't respond to Olaf. They were too busy staring at a cliff in front of them. They had a hit a dead end.

"What now?" Anna asked.

Kristoff sighed. "It's too steep," he said. "I've only got one rope, and you don't know how to climb mountains."

Anna put her hands on her hips. "Says who?" she countered, and headed straight for the mountain face.

Kristoff and Sven watched as Anna struggled to pull herself up the sheer slope.

"What are you doing?" Kristoff asked.

"I'm going to see my sister," Anna said, straining to secure a handhold or a foothold in the ice.

"You're going to kill yourself," Kristoff observed. "I wouldn't put my foot there."

Anna turned. "You're distracting me!" As soon as she put her foot down, it slipped and she nearly toppled over. Anna paused and took a deep breath. Kristoff was right. The mountain was too steep to climb, but she didn't want to give up.

"How do you know Elsa even wants to see you?" Kristoff asked.

"I'm just blocking you out 'cause I've got to concentrate here," she said.

Kristoff crossed his arms over his chest. "I'm just saying, most people who disappear into the mountains want to be alone."

"Nobody wants to be alone," Anna said, observing him. "Except maybe you."

"I'm not alone," Kristoff said. "I have friends."

"Oh, right, the love experts," Anna scoffed.

Kristoff was not amused. "Yes, the love experts!"

Anna turned to face the mountain again and started to climb. "Please tell me I'm almost there," she called over her shoulder. The air seemed thinner to her, and she was growing tired of holding on.

But Anna was only a couple of feet off the ground! Kristoff sighed and reached into his bag for climbing picks. "Hang on," he said.

"Not sure if this is going to solve the problem," Olaf called from around the side of a snow boulder.

"But I found a staircase that leads exactly where you want it to go."

Relief spread through Anna, and she dropped from her perch on the ice wall, yelling "Catch!" to Kristoff. She fell right into his arms. "Thanks," she said, grinning. "That was like some crazy trust exercise!"

The group formed a circle around a large rock formation, and there was Olaf, standing next to a shimmering frozen staircase. Looking up, they saw that it led to a huge and elaborate ice palace. Massive pillars of gleaming ice supported the structure, which was covered with a delicate pattern of crystalline snowflakes. Anna and Kristoff were awestruck.

"Talk about cut, color, and clarity," Kristoff said, admiring the ice. "I might cry."

"Go ahead. I won't judge," Anna said.

Anna approached the front door and pushed it open. She turned to Kristoff and Olaf and motioned for them to wait outside. She didn't want to risk upsetting Elsa. "The last time I introduced her to a guy, she froze everything," she explained. "Just give us a minute."

As soon as Anna left, Olaf began to count. "One, two, three, four . . ."

14

*A*nna cautiously entered Elsa's palace. She found herself in a huge room with an impressive winding staircase leading to a second floor. The palace was gorgeous, but it was absolutely still and eerily quiet.

"Elsa?" Anna called nervously. "It's me, Anna."

"Anna," Elsa replied. Anna followed the sound of her sister's voice and saw her at the top of the staircase. She was surprised by Elsa's new appearance.

"Elsa, you look beautiful," she said. "And this place is amazing."

Elsa smiled. "Thank you. I never knew what I was capable of."

Anna started up the stairs. "I'm sorry about what happened. If I'd known . . ."

"No, it's okay," said Elsa, backing away. "You don't have to apologize. But you should probably go, please."

Anna was startled. "But I just got here."

"You belong in Arendelle," Elsa explained. "I belong here. Alone. Where I can be who I am without hurting anybody."

"Actually, about that—" Anna began. But Olaf ran in, interrupting her. The minute was up, and he couldn't wait another second.

"Wait," said Elsa, wide-eyed. "What is that?"

Olaf ran up the staircase. "Hi, I'm Olaf, and I like warm hugs," he said. Suddenly, the little snowman felt shy. "You built me," he told Elsa. "You remember that?"

Elsa stared at him. "And you're alive?" she asked in wonder. She looked at her hands, amazed at her own power.

"I think so," Olaf replied.

"He's just like the one we built as kids," Anna said. "We were so close. We can be like that again."

More than anything, Elsa wanted that to be true. But the white streak in Anna's hair was a constant reminder of that night long ago when she hit Anna with her dangerous powers.

Elsa turned and headed back upstairs. "No, we can't," she said. "Goodbye, Anna."

"Elsa, wait!" Anna said. "Please don't shut me out again."

Anna ran to the upper floor and tried to reason with her sister. Now that Elsa's secret was out, Anna thought they could be happy together for the first time in forever.

But it wasn't that simple for Elsa. She was sure no one in Arendelle would ever accept her again. She couldn't hide her powers anymore—and she didn't want to! What if she injured someone? What if she hurt Anna? Elsa felt that if she could just keep to herself, no one would be hurt by her magic. But there was something Elsa didn't know.

"You kind of set off an eternal winter everywhere," Anna said.

"Everywhere?" said Elsa, shaken by the news.

Anna wanted to be encouraging. "It's okay, you can just unfreeze it."

Elsa looked away. "No, I can't. I don't know how," she admitted.

Anna wasn't worried. "Sure, you can. I know you can." Anna ran to her sister. She was sure they could work it out.

For her part, Elsa was having trouble keeping

her emotions under control. The news that she had accidentally put Arendelle into a deep freeze was very hard to bear. Maybe she *was* the monster that people thought she was. The walls of the palace started to ice over. Elsa wanted to get away from Anna. She backed farther up the stairs, and the banister frosted over as she passed.

But Anna kept pressing Elsa. "Everything will be all right," she insisted.

Elsa was torn. She did want to go home, she did want everything to be fine, but it just wasn't possible! Frustrated and upset, she exclaimed, "I can't!"

With those words, Elsa's bottled-up emotions rose to the surface. A wave of icy magic was released from her body, and it struck Anna right in the chest! Anna fell backward as Elsa gasped.

Olaf ran to Anna and helped her stand up. Kristoff entered the room and ran to Anna, as well.

"I'm okay," she said bravely. "I'm fine."

"I told you to stay away!" said Elsa in horror.

"No, I'm not giving up," Anna said. "I know we can figure this out together."

"How?" Elsa shouted. "What power do you have to stop this winter? To stop me?"

"I don't know," Anna said, tears welling up in her eyes. "But I'm not leaving without you!"

Heartbroken, Elsa looked at her sister. "Yes," she said. "You are." She waved a hand, and magic shimmered in the air. Suddenly, a giant snowman rose from the floor, conjured by her powers. The snowman grew and grew, until he towered over Anna and her friends.

"You made me a little brother!" Olaf exclaimed happily. He turned to the huge creature. "I'm going to name you Marshmallow!"

15

*M*arshmallow grabbed the unwanted visitors and tossed them down the icy steps. "Go home!" roared the snowman.

But Olaf remained in Marshmallow's arms, having come apart with all the jostling. "You are a lot stronger than I think you realize," he told the snow giant.

Marshmallow howled and threw Olaf, one piece at a time, down the mountain.

"Heads up!" Olaf's head shouted as it soared past Anna and Kristoff.

The head crashed into a snowbank.

"Olaf!" cried Anna, racing over to Olaf's head.

"Watch out for my butt!" he warned.

Anna and Kristoff jumped out of the way just as the rest of Olaf's body slammed into the snowbank.

Anna picked up a handful of snow and molded it into a ball. Then she flung it at the huge snowman.

"It's not nice to throw people!" she shouted angrily.

Marshmallow roared—and charged after them!

"All right, feisty-pants," Kristoff said to Anna. "Now you made him mad!"

"I'll distract him," Olaf said. "You guys go!"

Olaf's belly and butt took off in opposite directions. "No, not you guys!" he yelled to the two body balls, then sighed. "This just got a lot harder."

Anna and Kristoff slid down the mountain. When they reached the bottom, Marshmallow was already there!

"Look out!" Kristoff called.

They quickly got up and ran through a maze of trees and snowbanks, with Marshmallow close behind them.

"This way!" Anna shouted. She grabbed a stick and knocked the heavy snow off a tree. With the extra weight lifted, the tree snapped upright and knocked Marshmallow back. Anna and Kristoff laughed and ran ahead of the snowman. But Marshmallow was not giving up.

Anna and Kristoff continued to run until they reached the edge of a steep cliff.

"Whoa, stop!" Kristoff yelled.

Anna peered over the edge. "It's a hundred-foot drop," she said.

"It's two hundred," he countered. Taking a rope, Kristoff tied a loop around Anna's waist. Then he dug a U shape in the snow.

"What's that for?" Anna asked.

"I'm digging a snow anchor," Kristoff told her.

"Okay. What if we fall?" Anna said. She looked over the edge again.

"There's twenty feet of fresh powder down there," he answered. "It'll be like landing on a pillow." He paused, and then added, "Hopefully."

Anna's eyes widened.

Kristoff tied off the rope in the snow anchor. "Okay, Anna," he said. "On three . . ."

Anna moved closer to the edge.

"One, two . . . ," Kristoff counted. Just then, a tree sailed through the air. Marshmallow had thrown it at them!

"Tree!" Anna yelled. She jumped over the cliff, pulling Kristoff with her.

"What? Whoa!" Kristoff hollered as the two plummeted. Seconds later, the rope caught their fall and they were dangling in midair.

At that moment, Olaf emerged from the trees, a complete mess. His body parts were in the wrong order as he staggered toward the cliff.

"Oh, man, I am out of shape," he mumbled, winded from the chase. He quickly put himself back together properly. "There we go," he said. "Hey, Anna! Kristoff! Where'd you guys go?" He searched all around. "We totally lost Marshmallow back there!"

Marshmallow stepped forward and stood behind Olaf.

Olaf peered up and smiled. "Hey, we were just talking about you," he said. "All good things, all good things," he quickly added.

The big snowman roared and went for the snow anchor that held Kristoff and Anna. Olaf took action and jumped onto Marshmallow's leg. "No!" he shouted. Realizing he was no match for the giant, Olaf shrugged. "This is not making much of a difference, is it?"

Marshmallow shook off the little snowman and kicked him over the edge of the cliff. Olaf flew past the dangling Anna and Kristoff.

"Hang in there, guys!" he called.

A tug on the rope told Anna and Kristoff that

Marshmallow was pulling them back up to the ledge! They started spinning out of control. Kristoff reached down for Anna and hit his head on the cliff.

"Ugh!" he shouted.

Marshmallow pulled them almost to the top. "Don't come back!" he bellowed.

"We won't!" Anna answered. She reached up and cut the rope with a knife. She and Kristoff fell down, down, down . . . and landed in a deep pile of soft snow.

Suddenly, everything was quiet. "Hey, you were right," Anna said, sitting up and shaking the snow out of her hair. "Just like a pillow!" She looked over and saw Olaf.

"I can't feel my legs!" Olaf screamed, panicking as he stared at two feet coming through the snow in front of him. "I can't feel my legs!"

"That's because those are my legs," Kristoff said, sitting up just behind Olaf.

Suddenly, Olaf's lower body came running over. "Oh, hey," Olaf said to Kristoff. "Do me a favor and grab my butt."

Kristoff took Olaf's chatty head and slammed it onto his body.

"Oh, that feels better," Olaf said happily.

Sven walked over and sniffed Olaf's carrot nose.

"Hey, Sven!" Olaf greeted the reindeer and then turned toward Anna and Kristoff just before Sven could bite the carrot. "He found us!" He looked back at Sven. "Who's my cute little reindeer?" he cooed.

Kristoff pulled Olaf away from Sven. "Don't talk to him like that."

Then Kristoff went to help Anna. "You okay?" he asked, pulling her out of the snow.

"Whoa! Strong man," Anna said. "Okay, thank you." Anna's and Kristoff's eyes met. They held the gaze for a long moment and then looked away.

"How's your head?" Anna asked. She touched the spot where Kristoff had banged his head on the cliff.

"Ow!" he shouted. "I mean . . . it's fine. I've got a thick skull."

Anna giggled.

"I don't have a skull," Olaf remarked. "Or bones."

"So now what?" Kristoff asked Anna.

The question sent Anna into a panic. "I don't know! What am I going to do? Elsa threw me out, I can't go back to Arendelle with the weather like this, and then there's your ice business. . . ."

Kristoff felt bad for Anna, but he knew panicking wouldn't help. He tried to steer her back to their current situation. "Hey, don't worry about my ice business," he told her. "Worry about your hair."

Anna's hands flew to her head and she tried to smooth down her hair. "What? I just fell off a cliff," she said. "You should see your hair."

"No, yours is turning white," he said, concerned.

"White?" Anna cried. She grabbed her long braid just as another section of hair lost its color.

"It's because she struck you with her powers, isn't it?" Kristoff asked.

"Does it look bad?"

Kristoff thought for a moment. "No," he said.

Olaf popped up. "You hesitated," he said.

"No, I didn't," Kristoff said. He knew that Anna needed help. And he knew where to go—and who to ask. "Come on."

"Okay! Where are we going?" Olaf asked.

"To see my friends," Kristoff said.

Anna's eyebrows rose up. "The love experts?"

Olaf was surprised. "Love experts?"

"Yes," Kristoff answered. "They'll be able to fix this."

Anna followed Kristoff and Sven, with Olaf trailing behind. "How can you be so sure?" she asked.

"Because I've seen them do it before."

"I like to consider myself a love expert," Olaf said sweetly.

16

*F*ar down the mountain in Arendelle, the air was still frigid and snow blanketed the land. People wondered if warm weather would ever return. The fjord was frozen solid, and all the dignitaries who had arrived for Elsa's coronation were forced to stay since their ships were stuck. In the meantime, men and women were working hard to unload supplies from the marooned boats and haul them to the castle, where they could be stored and distributed.

Hans moved through the crowded village, handing out heavy cloaks. "Who needs a cloak?" he asked. "The castle is open. There's soup and hot glogg in the Great Hall," he said, referring to a special drink of hot wine.

"Arendelle is indebted to you, Your Highness," a woman said.

The Duke approached. "Prince Hans!" he said.

"Are we just expected to sit here and freeze while you give away all of Arendelle's tradeable goods?"

"Calm yourself," counseled Hans. "Princess Anna has given her orders."

The Duke went on. "Has it dawned on you that your princess may be conspiring with a wicked sorceress to destroy us all?"

"Do not question the princess," Hans responded forcefully. "She left me in charge, and I will not hesitate to protect Arendelle from treason."

The Duke was put in his place. "Treason? No, I— I . . . ," he stuttered.

Hans didn't have a chance to reply. At that moment, Anna's horse galloped into the village square.

"Whoa!" Hans called to the horse, catching his reins. "Easy, easy."

"Princess Anna's horse!" a man shouted. "What happened to her? Where is she?"

Panic grew among the villagers. Hans looked toward the North Mountain. "Princess Anna is in trouble!" he cried. "I need volunteers to go with me to find her."

A number of men immediately stepped forward. The Duke ordered his two huge guards to join the search party as well. But he gave them a little advice before they left.

"Should you encounter the queen," the Duke told his men quietly, "be prepared to put an end to this winter. Do you understand?"

The men nodded and smiled. They enjoyed a good fight.

Soon they all trailed Hans across the frozen fjord and up into the mountains.

· · ❯ ɔ · ❯ ——— ❀ ——— ᴄ· ᴄ❮· ·

In her ice palace at the top of the mountain, Elsa looked out the window and felt her own panic rising. She hadn't meant to hit Anna with her magic, and she wished she could take it back.

"Get it together," she told herself, trying to use all those strategies her parents had taught her years ago. "Control it. Don't feel, don't feel."

Just then, ice cracked behind her. Looking around, she realized a trail of ice had formed behind her— and it was going up the wall!

Frightened, she gave a sharp cry and continued working to keep herself under control. "Don't feel. Don't feel. DON'T FEEL!"

The ice on the floor began to change and grow into a series of sharp spikes. Alarmed, she glanced out the window. The wind was rising as the weather whipped up to match her feelings of worry.

··)》ᵓ·ᵓ》——✦——《ᵒ·ᵒ《··

Hans and his volunteers made their way through the snowy woods and braved the steep incline of the North Mountain. Some were on horseback, while others walked. Many of them carried torches and swords. The Duke's guards carried crossbows.

All around them, the storm was growing worse.

At the top of mountain, Hans led the group around the rocky cliffs, and eventually they came upon the ice palace. He turned to the men as they all gaped at the spectacular structure. "We're here to find Princess Anna," he reminded them. "Be on guard, but no harm is to come to the queen."

Suddenly, a mass of snow rose from the ground behind Hans. It was Marshmallow! The huge snowman refused to move away from the palace entrance. As the volunteers pressed forward, Marshmallow reacted quickly, knocking men to the ground. Hans rolled to safety and grabbed his sword.

Then Elsa, still upset from Anna's visit, stepped out onto her balcony to see what was happening. She was spotted by one of the Duke's guards. They ducked around Marshmallow's legs, raced into the palace, and charged up the stairs.

"Stay back!" Elsa warned. She didn't want her powers to hurt anyone. The men had their crossbows aimed at her. She held up her arms and summoned a wall of ice for protection.

But the Duke's guards kept coming. Desperate to keep them away, she waved her arms, and the wall of ice forced one of the attackers onto the balcony. He teetered on the edge, trapped.

The other guard was still coming after Elsa, with his crossbow ready to shoot. With another wave, Elsa created a series of icy spikes, pinning the man in place against the wall. The spikes came right up to his jaw, barely allowing him to breathe.

Outside the palace, Hans and his fighters continued to battle the powerful snowman. Hans swept Marshmallow's leg with his sword, forcing the snow giant to fall. Marshmallow rolled away and off a cliff. Hans and his men raced into the ice palace.

There, he immediately spotted the guard trapped

against the wall and the other one pushed to the very edge of the balcony. The man was just inches from falling to his death!

"Queen Elsa, no, please!" Hans called out. "Don't be the monster they fear you are!"

Elsa saw the fright in the guard's eyes and hesitated. With a start, she realized she had gone too far; this was exactly what she had worked so long to avoid. As she looked down at her hands, the wall of ice retreated. She had always tried to keep people safe, not put them in more danger—and now her self-control seemed to be dissolving entirely.

But as the icy spikes melted away from the Duke's other guard, he aimed his crossbow at Elsa. Hans acted quickly. He pushed the man's crossbow aside, causing it to shoot at the ceiling. The loose arrow hit the chandelier above Elsa, sending it crashing to the floor. Shards of ice flew through the air . . . and Elsa fell, knocked unconscious.

··>⟩·⟩>——❀·——<⟨·<⟨··

Hours later, Elsa's eyes fluttered open. She was in a stone room with one tiny window high on the wall letting a cold light into the room. Elsa rose from the bench where she lay—and realized that she could not bring her arms forward. Her hands were encased in thick coverings, which were connected to long chains and bolted to the floor. She could see out the window well enough, though, to know that she was back in Arendelle. She was imprisoned in the castle dungeon and could see the snow continuing to fall over the kingdom.

"No!" Elsa cried, looking out at her frozen kingdom. "What have I done?"

17

Kristoff and Sven led Anna and Olaf through a rocky area of the mountains, weaving through valleys and hills. Darkness had fallen, but the northern lights lit the sky with a green glow. Anna hoped Kristoff's friends wouldn't mind that they were stopping by so late.

Kristoff could see that Anna was shivering. "Are you cold?" he asked.

Anna grinned. "I'm fine." It made Anna feel better that Kristoff was concerned about her.

"Good," said Kristoff, coming to a halt. "Well, we made it. Meet my friends. They're more like family, actually."

Anna looked around, confused. It was a valley of rocks. "They're rocks," she pointed out.

"They're love experts," Olaf said.

"They're experts on everything, really," Kristoff

explained. He looked very serious.

Anna thought Kristoff had lost his mind. She started to back away. "Right. Well, thank you for your help, but I'm thinking I'm going to go. Now. Right now."

Suddenly, rocks began to roll toward them. Strange voices called out, saying, "Kristoff's home! Kristoff's home!" As Anna watched, the rocks rose from the ground one after another and transformed into trolls. Suddenly, they were surrounded!

Hulda pushed her way to the front, thrilled to see Kristoff. Clearly, she knew him well. "He's brought a girl!" she exclaimed with a grin.

The trolls climbed over each other to get a good look at Anna.

Hulda examined Anna. "Let me see. Bright eyes. Working nose. Strong teeth," she said. "Yes, she'll do nicely for our Kristoff."

Anna finally caught on. They believed she was Kristoff's girlfriend, and that he'd brought her to meet them! "Wait. No. H-he and I aren't . . . ," she stammered. "I mean, he's not, we're not . . ."

Kristoff jumped in. "What she means is, that's not why I brought her here. We need—"

A troll named Soren cut him off. "We know what you need," he said confidently. And with that, the trolls began to tell Anna all about Kristoff's shortcomings. According to them, he was a bit of a fixer-upper, but a little love would make everything right.

Anna wasn't sure how this information could help solve her problem, but Kristoff didn't seem worried. "Just do whatever they say, and you'll be fine," he advised her.

The trolls started dancing and singing about love being a force that brings out the best in everyone, even if people have made bad choices in the past. Their excitement was infectious, and Anna and Kristoff were soon swept up in the celebration. Anna actually enjoyed the dancing, and she even let the troll women decorate her hair. Before long, she and Kristoff were moved to an area where they stood in front of the entire troll crowd.

"Do you, Anna," a serious troll began, "take Kristoff to be your troll-fully wedded—"

"Wait! What?" Anna exclaimed.

"You're getting married," the troll said.

Just then, a mighty shiver shot through Anna and she collapsed. Kristoff caught her.

"I think someone has cold feet," Soren said.

Hulda sniffed. "Nervous jitters is all."

Kristoff held Anna tight. "No," he insisted. "Something's wrong."

Pabbie pushed his way through the crowd. "He's right. Something is wrong," he said. Pabbie walked up to Anna, took her hands, and looked into her weakened eyes. A shiver went through her body as he lifted a lock of her hair, which was now all white.

"Anna," Pabbie said in a low voice, "your life is in danger."

A hush fell over the trolls. Anna looked at Kristoff as Pabbie continued.

"There is ice in your heart, put there by your sister. If not removed . . . to solid ice you will freeze," he told her. "Forever."

"What? No!" Anna gasped.

Kristoff tried to stay calm. "So remove it, Pabbie," he said.

"I can't. If it were in her head, that would be easy," Pabbie said. "But only an act of true love can thaw a frozen heart."

"An act of true love?" Anna repeated.

"A true love's kiss, perhaps?" suggested a nearby troll.

Kristoff paused, thinking. "We've got to get you back to Hans," he said.

"Hans," Anna answered weakly. "Right. Hans."

Quickly, Kristoff scooped Anna into his arms and placed her on Sven's back. He climbed up behind her, nodding his thanks to the trolls.

Hulda sighed. "Ugh. We'll never get him married, Soren," she muttered.

"Someday, Hulda," Soren replied.

Kristoff took hold of Sven's reins. "Come on, Olaf!" he called.

"I'm coming!" Olaf shouted, grabbing Sven's tail. "Let's go kiss Hans!"

Sven turned and headed back toward Arendelle, breaking into a gallop as he left the trolls' valley. The sun began to rise. And one by one, the trolls turned back into stone.

⋯≫‧୭❯—❀—❮୧‧≪⋯

Hans carried a torch as he walked down the steps into the dungeon of Arendelle castle. He appeared in the doorway of Elsa's cell.

Elsa was gazing out the small window at Arendelle, now buried in snow and ice. She turned when she heard Hans enter. "Why did you bring me here?" Elsa asked.

"I couldn't just let them kill you," Hans told her.

Elsa glanced at her shackled hands. "But I'm a danger to Arendelle. Get Anna," she suggested.

"Anna has not returned," Hans said. "If you would just stop the winter and bring back summer . . . please."

Elsa stared at Hans with sad eyes. "Don't you see?" she said. "I can't. You have to tell them to let me go."

Hans walked back to the door. "I will do what I can," he said. Exiting the cell, he locked the door behind him.

Elsa looked down at her shackles. Ice was beginning to spread over them. And ice was forming along the edges of the floor. Elsa's emotions—and her powers—were again slipping out of her control.

18

Sven charged down the mountain at full speed with Kristoff and Anna on his back. Olaf slid down the trail next to them like a playful penguin.

Kristoff looked over at Anna. She was shivering and very pale. "Just hang in there," he said. "Come on, buddy. Faster!" he urged Sven.

When they arrived at Arendelle, Olaf shot ahead. "Wooo! I'll meet you guys at the castle," he said.

"Stay out of sight!" Kristoff called after him.

"I will!" Olaf yelled back as he disappeared down into the town. Kristoff watched him disappear from view. Then he heard a scream from someone who was obviously not expecting to see a talking snowman.

"Ah! It's alive!" the villager shrieked. So much for Olaf staying out of sight!

At the castle gates, a soldier soon spotted the reindeer and the two riders.

"It's Princess Anna!" he shouted.

Anna struggled to get off Sven.

"I've got you," Kristoff said, helping her off the reindeer.

Anna was very weak. Her eyes lifted to meet Kristoff's. "Are you going to be okay?" she asked.

"Don't worry about me," Kristoff said. Quickly, two servants rushed over to help Anna. "You need to get her to Prince Hans," Kristoff told them.

"You poor girl, you're freezing," the older servant said. "Let's get you inside. Let's get you warm."

As the servants whisked Anna away, Kristoff stood watching. Sven looked at his friend, unsure what he would do next. Then the castle door closed, shutting Kristoff out.

··⟩⟩·⟩⟩——❀——⟨⟨·⟨⟨··

In the castle library, Hans was meeting with dignitaries and soldiers, discussing the fate of Arendelle's queen.

"I'm going back out to look for Anna," Hans told them. "No one is to go near the queen until I get back."

"Prince Hans," a man said. "You cannot risk going out there again. Arendelle needs you."

Hans sank into a chair. "But if anything happens to Princess Anna . . ."

"If anything happens to Princess Anna," another dignitary said, "you are all Arendelle has left. Please."

The door flew open, and the two servants brought Anna into the room.

"Anna!" Hans exclaimed as she fell into his arms. "You're so cold."

"Hans, you have to kiss me," she managed to say.

"What?" he asked.

"Now!" Anna said desperately.

Hans was a bit taken aback. "Slow down," he said.

The servants smiled, realizing that Anna and Hans needed to be alone. "We'll give you two some privacy," said one, backing away. Everyone in the room followed him out.

Once they were alone, Hans turned to Anna. "What happened out there?" he asked.

"Elsa struck me with her powers," she said softly.

"You said she'd never hurt you."

Anna lowered her eyes. "I was wrong," she said. "She froze my heart, and only an act of true love can save me."

19

Anna's body felt even colder than when she was out in the storm. But it was a relief to tell Hans everything, to know that he could help her.

After hearing the whole tale, Hans looked at her with a tender smile. "A true love's kiss," he said pensively. He leaned in close, ready to kiss her. Anna lifted her chin and closed her eyes in anticipation. Then he stopped.

"Oh, Anna," he said. "If only somebody loved you."

"What?" Anna said in shock.

Hans rose to his feet and walked away. He stood in front of the window, looking out over the kingdom. "As thirteenth in line in my own kingdom, I didn't stand a chance," he told her. "I knew I'd have to marry into the throne somewhere."

Anna could barely lift her head. "What? What are you talking about?" she asked.

"As heir, Elsa was preferable, of course," Hans continued. "But no one was getting anywhere with her. But you . . ." He trailed off with a small smile.

"Hans?" Anna said, growing concerned.

"Like your sister said," he told her. "You were so desperate for love, you were willing to marry me just like that." He walked over to a table and grabbed a pitcher of water. Then he moved closer to the fire. "I figured after we married, I'd have to stage a little accident for Elsa." He poured the water on the fire, putting it out.

Anna reached out to stop him, but she was too weak and once again fell to the floor. "Hans, no, stop!" she cried.

Ignoring her plea, Hans took the fire poker and smothered the remaining embers. A cold draft filled the room. "But then she doomed herself, and you were dumb enough to go after her," he snickered.

"Please," Anna begged.

Hans laughed. "All that's left now is to kill Elsa and bring back summer."

A sense of despair engulfed Anna as she realized the depth of Hans's cruelty. "You're no match for Elsa," she said bravely.

Hans looked down at Anna. "No, *you're* no match for Elsa," he told her. "I, on the other hand, am the hero who is going to save Arendelle from destruction." He strode to the door.

"You won't get away with this," Anna said fiercely.

"Oh, I already have," Hans said with a nasty grin. He walked out, locking the door tight.

Anna tried to get up from the floor, but she was too weak. She could feel the cold taking the last of her strength.

"Please, somebody," she called out hoarsely. "Help!" She looked around the dark room and knew she was totally alone. "Please, please," she whispered.

And then she collapsed.

-->>ᵒ ·ᵒ>— ❀ —<ᵒ· ᶜ<<··

Hans left Anna and went to the council chamber where the Duke and other dignitaries were gathered.

"It's getting colder by the minute," the Duke said. "Forget starving; we'll soon freeze to death."

Hans fell into a chair, looking weak and grief-stricken.

"Prince Hans!" a dignitary said, reaching out to him gently.

Hans lowered his head and chuckled to himself. He had sat down on the throne. His plan was moving along perfectly. Pretending to be full of remorse, Hans said, "Princess Anna is . . . dead."

"What?" the other men exclaimed.

"How could this happen?" one of the dignitaries asked.

Hans shook his head slowly. "She was killed by Queen Elsa."

"No!" the Duke shouted.

With his head in his hands, Hans played the part of a grieving man. "We said our wedding vows . . . before she died in my arms."

"There can be no doubt now," the Duke declared. "Queen Elsa is a monster!"

"Prince Hans," stated one of the dignitaries. "Arendelle looks to you."

Hans nodded grimly, but he was secretly elated. Never in his wildest dreams could he have plotted his ascent to the throne so gloriously. "With a heavy heart, I charge Queen Elsa with treason and sentence her to death," he declared.

··❯❯··❯·❯━━❀━━❮··❮··❮❮··

In her dungeon cell, Elsa stood by the window. The snow was cascading down heavily. She wondered where Anna was at that moment. Anna would never be able to survive this storm.

Maybe I am a monster, she thought. Hans's words haunted her. Her powers had done nothing but cause great trouble for the kingdom.

Elsa knew that she had to leave Arendelle so she wouldn't do any more harm. As her eyes welled up with tears, she looked down at her shackles. They were completely frozen, and suddenly, they broke open. Then, with a thunderous crash, ice broke through the dungeon walls, splitting them apart as Elsa's emotions overwhelmed her mind and heart. Realizing she could escape, Elsa hurried through the gaping hole in the wall.

Hans heard the noise and ran down to the dungeon. The Duke and his guards were already there.

"What happened?" Hans asked.

"The queen has escaped," the Duke replied, gazing through the opening in the wall.

20

$\mathcal{T}$he howling winds pushed against Kristoff as he headed back up the mountain, away from Arendelle. He adjusted his goggles and wrapped his scarf tightly around his face.

Sven was lagging behind. The reindeer looked longingly back at Arendelle and the castle. He shook his head and whinnied. Kristoff kept walking, ignoring him. Sven charged ahead, passed Kristoff, and then stopped in front of him. He faced him and looked Kristoff directly in the eye.

"What is it, buddy?" Kristoff asked.

The reindeer nudged his antlers into Kristoff's side.

"Hey, watch it," Kristoff said, annoyed. "What's wrong with you?"

Sven shook his head and wiggled his mouth.

"I don't understand you when you talk that way,"

Kristoff told him. In a flash, Sven bucked Kristoff and lifted him up with his antlers. "Hey! Stop it!" Kristoff shouted. "Put me down."

Sven dropped him straight into the snow, hard.

"No, Sven," Kristoff said. "We're not going back."

Sven snorted his disapproval.

"She's with her true love." Kristoff saw Sven's doubt. He glanced back at the kingdom to make his point. But to his surprise, he saw a strange new storm swirling above the castle. He could see dark clouds forming, and more ice on the castle walls, putting it into an even deeper freeze. "Anna!" he cried.

Instantly, Kristoff changed his course and took off running toward Arendelle. Sven scrambled and raced up behind him. He ducked his head and lifted Kristoff with his antlers, then threw him onto his back. The duo raced down the hillside.

⋯≫⋅≫──❀──≪⋅≪⋯

Anna was curled up on the floor of the library. She had made it to the door but was now too weak to stand. No one could hear her whispered cries for help. She was so cold—and her heart ached.

At that moment, the door handle jiggled. Anna

was barely able to raise her head to see who it was. The lock clicked. Anna could see a carrot wedged into the keyhole. . . .

Suddenly, the door flew open. It was Olaf! The snowman pulled his carrot nose out of the lock and put it back into the middle of his face. He was very proud of himself, but his happiness melted the moment he saw Anna.

"Anna, no!" he called. He ran to the fireplace and struck a match. In seconds there was a large, roaring fire.

"Olaf," Anna said. "Get away from there!"

"Whoa!" Olaf exclaimed, taking in the sight and feel of the fire. He was a little scared, but he couldn't resist the warmth coming from the fireplace. "So that's heat," he said. "I gotta say, I still like it!" He hurried over to Anna and brought her closer to the fire. "So, where's Hans? What happened to your kiss?"

"I was wrong about him," Anna said. "It wasn't true love."

Olaf didn't want to believe it. "But we rode all the way here," he said.

"Please, Olaf," Anna managed to say. "You can't stay here. You'll melt."

"I'm not leaving until we find some other act of true love to save you," Olaf said. He sat down next to Anna. "Got any ideas?"

Anna sighed heavily. "I don't even know what love is anymore."

"That's okay," Olaf said. "I do." He sat up a little taller. "Love is putting someone else's needs before yours—like, you know how Kristoff brought you back here to Hans and left you forever?"

"Kristoff loves me?" Anna asked. Her eyes widened.

Olaf nodded. "You really don't know anything about love, do you?"

Anna looked at Olaf. He was dripping from head to toe! "Olaf, you're melting!" she cried.

"Some people are worth melting for," he said. His face was quickly losing its shape. Olaf tried to push up his sagging head. He ran and sat behind Anna, trying to escape the fire's heat. "Just maybe not right this second."

A window across the room blew open and a cold gust of wind swept through. Anna shuddered. Olaf ran to the window to shut it. "Don't worry," he said. "I've got it. We're gonna get through . . ." He stopped talking and stared out the window. He leaned forward and squinted at the horizon. "Hang on, just one second. I'm getting something!"

He reached through the open window and grabbed an icicle off the window ledge. He flipped the icicle around and used it as a telescope. "Hey, Kristoff and Sven!" he shouted when he realized who was running toward the castle. He turned to Anna excitedly. "They're coming back this way!"

"They are?" Anna asked. She tried to stand up to see for herself.

"Wow, he's moving really fast!" Olaf said. "Huh, I guess I was wrong. I guess Kristoff doesn't love you enough to leave you behind."

"Help me up," Anna said, struggling. "Please."

"No," Olaf told her. "You need to stay by the fire and keep warm."

Anna was adamant. "I need to get to Kristoff."

"Why?" Olaf asked. Then he paused. "Oh, I know why! There's your act of true love right there, riding across the fjords like a valiant, pungent reindeer king!" He reached for Anna. "Come on!"

Sheets of ice began to break through the library walls. The cracks grew across the walls, and the room began to collapse. Anna and Olaf hurried out of the library just in time. Together, they struggled to make it through the hallway, dodging ice as it appeared in their path.

"Back this way," Olaf said, pulling Anna. But every path they tried was blocked by ice! "We're trapped!" he shouted.

Anna spun around and spotted a way out. She took Olaf's hand and they made their way over to a window, broke the glass, and slid down an icy ramp. Olaf picked up more snow as he went. They landed safely outside the castle and took off toward Kristoff.

21

$\mathcal{T}$he winds were picking up as the storm raged throughout Arendelle. The snow continued to fall, and the air was frigid. The ice blocks in the fjord were beginning to shift, which made walking on the frozen surface dangerous.

The snow hit Anna's face hard, blinding her, but she and Olaf continued. She held her hand up to shield her eyes when she reached the shore. It broke her heart to see the fjord waters frozen into solid blocks and the ships turned on their sides.

"Kristoff!" she called out weakly. She couldn't see him, but she knew he was coming over the fjord— and she knew he was her last chance for survival. The ice was still spreading through her heart, making her weaker and weaker. She was determined, but was losing strength with each step.

The snow was swirling wildly now, covering

everything. "Whoa!" Olaf cried as the wind lifted him up and took him from Anna.

Not far away, but completely engulfed in the snowstorm, Kristoff was riding on Sven's back, racing desperately toward Anna. As he passed over the fjord, a ship that was wedged in the thick ice in front of him began to shift and wobble. "Come on! Come on!" Kristoff urged Sven.

At that moment, the ice in front of Kristoff shifted again and caused the ship to drop, splintering the surface. Sven bravely jumped over the frigid waters and bucked his rider off to safety. Then the reindeer fell into the water.

"Sven!" Kristoff screamed. "Sven!"

With a mighty effort, Sven leaped out of the water and landed safely on a floating piece of ice. He nodded, signaling that he was all right.

"Good boy," Kristoff called. He turned back to find Anna.

··❯·❯·❯———❀———❮·❮··❮··

Hans was also out on the frozen fjord, struggling through the storm. He was pursuing Elsa, however—and he nearly had her. "Elsa!" he yelled loudly through the howling winds. "You can't run from this!"

"Don't try to stop me," Elsa called back to him. "Just take care of my sister."

"Your sister?" Hans laughed. "She returned from the mountain weak and cold. She said you froze her heart."

Elsa gasped. "No!" She was overwhelmed by what her powers had done. Her worst fears had come true.

"I tried to save her," Hans lied. "But it was too late. Her skin was ice. Her hair turned white. Your sister is dead because of you."

Elsa dropped to her knees and put her head in her hands.

The storm stopped abruptly in response to Elsa's overwhelming despair. The winds and the driving snow ceased, leaving snowflakes suspended in the air.

In the sudden stillness, Kristoff finally spotted Anna. She was clutching her chest and her skin was pale, almost white. Her strength was decreasing with each passing moment.

Barely able to speak, she uttered his name and fell to her knees. "Kristoff."

"Anna! Anna!" Kristoff called desperately as he ran toward her.

In the quiet air, the people of Arendelle gathered at the shore, staring out at the frozen fjord. The view was finally clear, and they could see their queen kneeling on the ice, her head bowed. Prince Hans stood just behind her.

22

$\mathcal{T}$hough Anna could barely move, she lifted her head to see Kristoff coming toward her. But nearby, in the other direction, she suddenly caught sight of something else—something she could hardly believe. Was that her sister? Could Elsa also be out on the ice? Anna tried to focus.

Then she realized that Hans was standing over Elsa, who knelt on the ice, her face buried in her hands. Horrified, Anna watched as Hans drew his sword and raised it over her sister's head. He was taking his time, almost smiling with anticipation.

Anna knew that kissing Kristoff was her last hope for survival, but she couldn't bear to see Elsa in danger. With great difficulty, she turned away from Kristoff and moved toward her sister.

"Elsa!" she cried. With a final surge of energy, Anna lunged, using every remaining ounce of her strength. She threw herself in front of Elsa to block Hans's blow. "NO!" she shouted.

In that instant, Anna's entire body froze, turning into solid ice. Hans's sword came down at full strength on her body. The sword shattered! Hans reacted in angry astonishment as jagged pieces of steel fell into the snow.

At the sound of the sword, Elsa turned . . . and saw Anna's frozen body, one arm raised to shield her sister.

"Anna!" Elsa cried. She jumped up and threw her arms around her unseeing sister. "Oh, Anna," she said, weeping. "No, please, no!" Elsa sobbed, hugging the frozen figure.

Behind her, Hans was fuming. He quickly picked up his broken sword and started to swing it at Elsa, but Kristoff ran at him just in time. He hit Hans right on the jaw and knocked him down. There would be no second blows for Hans.

Olaf ventured forward, looking up at the sisters. He was shocked to see Anna so still, without movement or life. "Anna?" he asked sadly. He stepped back as Elsa hugged her sister and cried.

Kristoff, Sven, and Olaf all bowed their heads.

So did the dignitaries and citizens of Arendelle, watching from the shore. A somber silence fell over the kingdom.

Suddenly, as Elsa hugged her sister, drops of water began to form at the tips of Anna's fingers. Then her arm began to bend. Anna was beginning to thaw!

"Anna!" Elsa exclaimed.

"Elsa . . . ," Anna murmured. She opened her eyes and smiled lovingly at her sister. Elsa laughed with joy.

"You sacrificed yourself for me?" Elsa asked in wonder.

Still weak, Anna replied simply, "I love you."

Olaf gasped. "An act of true love will thaw a frozen heart," he said. Anna's sacrifice had saved her own life!

Elsa found herself turning Olaf's words over in her mind as she slowly realized their full meaning. "Love will thaw. . . . Love. Of course!" she said. She hugged Anna again and laughed.

"Of course what?" Olaf asked. Elsa took a step back and raised her hands above her head, and the snow drifted back up to the sky! Next, the ground began to shake and move. The ice and snow began to melt. The fjord waters thawed and a boat rose, lifting Elsa and the others onto its deck. Soon all the boats in the fjord were returned to their upright positions. Elsa waved her arms one more time and revealed a sunny sky! The warmth of a summer's day spread across the kingdom in one joyous moment.

All of Arendelle cheered!

"Hands down, this is the best day of my life!" Olaf exclaimed. But the snowman was again starting to melt. "And," he added, "quite possibly the last."

Elsa looked over at the dripping, sagging snowman. "Oh, Olaf," she said kindly. "Hang on, little guy." She waved a hand over Olaf and surrounded him with a swirl of cold air. Olaf quickly refroze and looked like himself again. Best of all, he now had a permanent little snow cloud above his head, to keep him from melting ever again.

"Ha!" he exclaimed. "How are we doing this?"

Hans climbed to his feet, still dazed from Kristoff's punch, and turned to Anna. "B-but she froze your heart," he stammered. He thought Anna had frozen to death back in the library.

"The only frozen heart around here is yours," Anna replied fiercely. Then, with all her might, she punched him in the face. Hans fell backward into the water.

Anna grinned. She was feeling warmer already. She caught sight of Kristoff and smiled. Then she hugged Elsa again. The sisters held each other tight. Neither one wanted to let go.

23

Summer returned to Arendelle, and the waters in the fjord were full of boats moving cargo and people. Hans sat locked in a cage on the deck of a ship preparing to return to the Southern Isles.

"I'll return this scoundrel to his country," a dignitary told the royal handler. "We shall see what his twelve brothers think of his behavior!"

Nearby, Arendelle soldiers were leading the Duke and his two guards to their ship.

"This is unacceptable," the Duke protested. "I am innocent! I'm a victim of fear. I demand to see the queen!"

"Oh, right," the royal handler told him. "I have a message from the queen: 'Arendelle will henceforth and forever no longer do business of any sort with Weaseltown.'"

"Weselton!" shouted the Duke. "It's Weselton!"

In the village, Anna hurried through the streets, pulling a blindfolded Kristoff behind her. "Come on, come on," she called to him.

Anna led Kristoff straight into people and almost slammed him into a pole. "You're not a very good blindfold guide," he told her. Finally, they stopped.

"Here we are!" Anna said. She pulled off Kristoff's blindfold. Before them sat a beautiful new sled. "I owe you a sled!"

Kristoff was taken aback. "Are you serious?" he said. "No. I can't accept this."

Anna laughed. "You have to. No returns. Queen's orders. She's named you the official Arendelle ice master and deliverer."

"That's not a thing," said Kristoff with a smile.

"Sure it is!" Anna said. "And it even has a cup holder. Do you like it?"

Kristoff hugged Anna. "Like it?" he asked. "I love it. I could kiss you!" Kristoff looked into Anna's eyes and suddenly felt bashful. "I mean, I'd like to. May I? I mean, may we? Wait—what?"

Anna leaned over and gave Kristoff a quick kiss. "We may," she said.

Kristoff smiled. Then he leaned in and kissed Anna

right back. But this time it was a real kiss, sweet and romantic, and perfect for Anna.

Not far away, Olaf was happily enjoying the summer weather with the help of his little snow cloud. He held a big bouquet of flowers up to his nose and took a deep sniff. Suddenly, he sneezed—and his carrot nose shot off his face!

Sven was standing nearby, and with a quick movement of his head, the reindeer reached out and caught the carrot in his mouth. For a moment, it looked like Sven might chomp down on his favorite food. But instead, he gave the carrot back to Olaf, who happily popped it back onto his face.

Just past Olaf, Anna saw something else that brought a smile to her face. The gates to the castle were wide open. Elsa stood in the courtyard. All around her, people were putting on ice skates. And the parts of the castle that had been destroyed earlier were now fully repaired—with ice!

"Are you ready?" Elsa was asking the crowd. She raised her arms, swirled them in the air, and created a beautiful ice rink!

Anna ran to her sister. "The gates are open," she said. "I like it."

Elsa put an arm around Anna. "Let's never close them again." Then, with a smile, she pulled Anna onto the ice so the two could skate around the rink, together at last.

Behind them, Sven ventured out onto the ice, too. But his skating didn't come so easily. His legs slipped and twisted as he struggled to keep his balance. Anxious for his friend, Kristoff chased after Sven, awkwardly trying to keep him upright.

Last came Olaf, who slid over to Anna and Elsa. Together, they all skated happily across the ice. Summer—as well as love and happiness—had finally returned to Arendelle.